What Is Heaven Like?

BEVERLY LEWIS

ILLUSTRATED BY

Pamela Querin

BETHANY BACKYARD®

What Is Heaven Like?

Text © 2006 by Beverly Lewis

Illustrations © 2006 by Pamela Querin

Design: Lookout Design, Inc.

Published by Bethany House Publishers
11400 Hampshire Avenue South
Bloomington, Minnesota 55438

Bethany House Publishers is a division of Baker Publishing Group, Grand Rapids, Michigan.

Printed in China.

ISBN-13: 978-0-7642-0184-4
ISBN-10: 0-7642-0184-0

Library of Congress Cataloging-in-Publication data applied for.

To Kailynn Therese,
our adorable and
inquisitive granddaughter—
the reason for this book.
—B.L.

For my family and friends
who helped bring to life the
characters in this book.
For Steve Baldwin and for the Scotts.
—P.Q.

IT RAINED SO HARD TODAY I wondered if the sun would ever shine again. The gray sky looked the way I felt inside. Sad.

When the rain finally stopped, I went out and climbed up the long ladder to my tree house. I sat there, missing Grandpa, and I wondered about heaven.

My big sister came out and sat with me. We didn't say much for a long time, just stared up at the sky together.

"Look!" I said, pointing, surprised to see a rainbow.

"You know what a rainbow means, don't you?" my sister asked. "It reminds us of God's promise never to flood the earth again."

Suddenly I remembered a promise Grandpa had made to me. Before he died he said, *"Don't be too sad. We'll see each other again someday."*

I asked what he meant, but Grandpa didn't have the chance to answer all my questions. So now I'm more curious than ever about heaven.

"There are many rooms in my Father's house.
If this were not true, I would have told you."

JOHN 14:2

After school the next day, my sister and I walked to the park. "What's heaven like?" I asked.

She smiled and raced me to the swings. "All the streets are made of shiny gold," she said. "And there are gates with giant pearls. Oh…and lots of angels, too."

"Will our house in heaven look like the one we live in now?" I asked. I stared hard at the clouds, and they became a gleaming white castle.

"Why do you want to know?" asked my sister.

"Because Grandpa's there. And I miss him…a whole bunch."

She stopped swinging and looked at me. "I do, too."

"We want you to know what happens to those who die.
We don't want you to be sad, as other people are.
They don't have any hope."

1 THESSALONIANS 4:13

The next day I saw the mail carrier coming up the street. "Has anyone ever sent a letter to someone in heaven?" I asked him.

Mr. Nelson shook his head. "Well, no. I think heaven's just a little too far away for that." He pointed to the sky. "It's past the moon and the Milky Way, too."

"You build your palace high in the heavens. You make the clouds serve as your chariot. You ride on the wings of the wind."

PSALM 104:3

At school I spied the playground teacher. "What's heaven like?" I asked.

Miss Birch smiled. "Let's see. I think for a boy like you, heaven might be a place where you could stay outside and play all the time. Skateboarding, swimming, riding bikes . . . without ever getting tired."

"*All* day?" I asked.

"Every day," she said with a twinkle in her eye. "And all night, too, if you want."

"The city does not need the sun or moon to shine on it.
God's glory is its light . . . . There will be no more night."

REVELATION 21:23, 22:5

During library time, I asked the librarian, "What's heaven like?"

Mrs. Turner lowered her glasses and leaned close. "I think it will be a happy place with lots of people who love you." Turning, she placed her finger over her lips and shushed two boys who were talking.

"Will we have to be quiet in heaven, too?" I asked.

She smiled and whispered back, "No, I think there will be plenty of joyful noise."

"Blessed are you who are sad now. You will laugh." LUKE 6:21

After school I ran to catch up with the ice-cream truck. "Is there yummy food in heaven?" I asked the driver.

Tyler grinned at me. "The best ever."

"Will I be able to eat whatever I want…whenever I want to?" I asked.

"Sure! And everything will be good for you, too." He handed me a Fudgsicle— my favorite.

"On each side of the river stood the tree of life,
bearing twelve crops of fruit." REVELATION 22:2

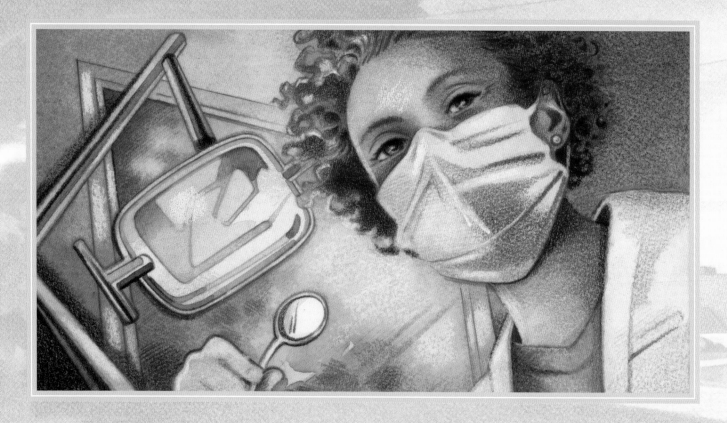

The next day I had my teeth cleaned and checked. I asked the dentist, "Will I ever get cavities in heaven?"

Doctor Anne looked at me and shook her head. "Your teeth will be strong and healthy," she said.

"No toothaches?" I asked.

"Never."

"There will be no more crying or pain.
Things are no longer the way they used to be."

REVELATION 21:4

On Saturday I watched the zookeeper feed the giraffes. "Are there animals in heaven?" I asked.

He chuckled and tossed a bundle of hay high into the feeding racks. "I can't imagine God's house without a fine puppy dog, can you?"

I thought of my own cuddly kitten and my sister's chirpy hamster. "Well…" I said. "I guess not."

"God created all the animals in the first place," he said. "So I wouldn't be surprised to find they live in heaven, too."

"[God] made all kinds of livestock. He made all kinds of creatures that move along the ground. And God saw that it was good."

GENESIS 1:25

When I got home, I ran next door to see Mrs. Johnson working in her garden. "What is heaven like?" I asked.

She wiped a smudge of dirt off her cheek. "I think it's the most wonderful place ever, filled with perfect flowers that never wilt. And not a single weed!"

"Does it smell good there?" I asked.

"Well, have you ever pushed your nose into a rose?" she asked. "Or sniffed a honeysuckle bush in full bloom?"

I nodded. "They smell just like Mom's perfume."

She tapped me on the nose and said, "I believe heaven is surely a sweet-smelling place."

"Through us, God spreads the knowledge of Christ everywhere like perfume."

2 CORINTHIANS 2:14

After supper, I helped Mom carry dishes to the sink. "I've been asking lots of
people about heaven," I told her. "The mailman, Miss Birch, my dentist…"

Mom stopped what she was doing. "Honey, remember you can always come to
Dad or me with questions, okay?" She gave me a hug. "We can look in the Bible
for answers, too. What would you like to know about heaven?"

"God has breathed life into all of Scripture.
It is useful for teaching us what is true."

2 TIMOTHY 3:16

I sat down, holding my kitty. "How do we get there?" I asked. "Mr. Nelson says heaven is far away."

Mom sat near me and smoothed back my hair. "Well, he's right, but it won't seem too far when it's our time to go there. We'll just close our eyes and wake up in heaven. Or if we are still living when the Lord returns, He will take us there himself."

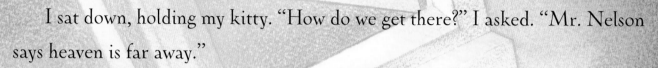

"We who are still alive and are left will be caught up
together with them.... We will meet the Lord in the air.
And we will be with him forever."

1 THESSALONIANS 4:17

At bedtime Dad came to pray with me. "Mom says you're asking questions about heaven."

"I miss Grandpa," I said, looking at the picture of him and Grandma on my bookcase. "Will Grandma die, too? Will you and Mom?"

Dad kissed my forehead. "Someday all of us will. Even you. But even though our bodies wear out during our years here on earth, our spirits will live forever."

"So part of me will keep on living?" I asked.

"That's right," Dad said. "God will give you a new body that won't grow old or get sick or ever die."

"He has the power to bring everything under his control. By his power he will change our earthly bodies. They will become like his glorious body."

PHILIPPIANS 3:21

After church the next day, we ate dinner at Grandma's house, then sang silly songs after dessert.

Later, I snitched two extra cookies, and Grandma caught me. "I guess no one will be naughty in heaven," I said, watching her face carefully.

She shook her head. "There is no room for even the smallest sin where God lives," Grandma said. "Though we all make plenty of mistakes here on earth." She gave me a squeeze. "You're welcome to the cookies, sweetie, but how about asking first next time?"

I nodded, my face warm. "I'm sorry, Grandma." Then I asked, "Are you ever sad about Grandpa?"

She glanced out the window, and I saw a sudden tear in her eye. "I miss his tender hugs and his crooked smile, yes. But most of all, I miss our talks."

"But you'll be with him again in heaven someday."

She smiled. "Yes, dear one."

"What do you think he's doing now?" I asked.

"Oh, your grandpa was never one to sit still for long. I'm sure he's keeping busy, having a never-ending adventure."

I felt real happy for Grandpa but awful sad for me.

"Only what is pure will enter.... Only those whose names are written in the Lamb's Book of Life will enter the city."

REVELATION 21:27

"I wish I could visit Grandpa," I said.

Grandma sat quietly, and then she said, "You'll see Grandpa again when it's your turn to go to heaven. But I think you have some important things to do *here* first. Just as we all do."

I thought about that. "Will the angels keep him company until I get there?"

"Oh yes. And there are lots of people, too, who have been eagerly waiting to see him." Grandma touched my cheek. "Grandpa is not lonely at all."

"Will I look like myself in heaven?" I asked.

She laughed softly. "Well, sure. How else will I know you?"

"That's good," I said. "So, when I go to heaven, will Grandpa be able to find me?"

"Yes, and I know he'll be so excited to see you again."

"Be glad and jump for joy.
You will receive many blessings in heaven."

LUKE 6:23

"Does Grandpa still pray a lot?" I asked, touching his worn Bible.

Grandma's face lit up. "I think so, but now he can talk to God face-to-face."

"Wow! Grandpa must love that!"

"You're right. I'm sure being that close to our heavenly Father is like opening a special present every single day."

I closed my eyes, thinking very hard. Knowing that God was spending time with Grandpa—and that He would do the same with me someday—that was the best promise of all.

*"We will see him as he really is. He is pure.
All who hope to be like him make themselves pure."*

1 JOHN 3:2-3

"How do I know if I'll go to heaven when I die?" I asked.

Grandma smiled. "God's only son, the Lord Jesus, came to our world as a tiny baby. Then, when Jesus grew to be a man—when it was just the right time—He died to take away our sins."

"God must love us a lot to let His Son do that."

"He certainly does." Grandma pulled her chair closer to me. "And God wants us to love Him back, but the choice is ours. We can either obey Him or go our own way. If you believe in Jesus—and trust Him to forgive your sins— you can be sure you are going to heaven."

I reached for her hand. "I think heaven will be the best and happiest place to live, don't you?"

Grandma nodded. "Imagine the most exciting day—like your birthday or how you felt the first time you hit a home run—well, that's only a small peek into what heaven will be like, I'm sure."

"*Anyone who hears my word and believes him who sent me has eternal life. He will not be found guilty. He has crossed over from death to life.*"

JOHN 5:24

"No eye has seen, no ear has heard, no mind has known
what God has prepared for those who love him."

1 CORINTHIANS 2:9

"I know a lot more about heaven now," I said.
"It's God's promise to me… to all of us. Just like
Grandpa promised we'll see each other again!"

"I will take you to be with me.
Then you will also be where I am."

JOHN 14:3

TEACHING YOUR CHILD ABOUT HEAVEN

You don't need to wait until a loved one dies to begin teaching your child about heaven. Children are naturally curious about their heavenly home—as we all are! Certainly, when a beloved relative or friend dies, the questions multiply as well as the sadness we experience. The purpose of this book is to bring hope to young hearts and to help answer some of those questions.

Undoubtedly, it will not answer all of them. Not even the wisest theologian knows everything about heaven. But you can address your child's questions with age-appropriate facts about what you do know and what the Bible teaches.

Parents often struggle with questions about death, concerned they will frighten their little ones. But typically, children are less upset by the truth than by the unknown. If your child asks about your own mortality, for example, perhaps say, "We will all die someday, but I hope it's not for a very long time." If your child sees you crying and asks why, you might say, "I am sad because I miss Grandma, but I know she is happy in heaven." If children are discouraged and wonder why God allows people to die, a truthful yet tender answer can be simply, "Death is hard to understand. But the Bible says those who believe in the Lord Jesus will live with Him forever—and I trust Jesus."

God, in Scripture, assures us of all we *need* to know (though perhaps not all we'd *like* to know) about heaven and life after death. The Scriptures in this book are only a few of the many helpful—and hopeful—insights God has given to encourage us and build our faith. If you are interested in learning more about heaven, there are a number of other resources available. Of course, the Bible is the best source for what we can learn and trust about heaven. A good concordance or one of the many online Bible search engines can help in your study.

As you seek to teach your family about heaven, may your own faith be strengthened, and if you are grieving yourself, may you be comforted by God's peace and the promise of our eternal home.

Beverly Lewis